The Boxcar Children Mysteries

THE MYSTERY OF THE MIDNIGHT DOG

created by
GERTRUDE CHANDLER WARNER

Illustrated by Hodges Soileau

ALBERT WHITMAN & Company
Morton Grove, Illinois

ISBN 0-8075-5476-6

9 10 8

Contents

THE MYSTERY OF THE MIDNIGHT DOG

CHAPTER 1

Kudzu and Ghost Finders

"Look! It looks just like a dinosaur!" Six-year-old Benny Alden pointed out the window of the car.

Henry, Jessie, and Violet Alden looked where their younger brother was pointing, and Watch, their dog, sat up and put his paws on the edge of the window. Only Grandfather Alden didn't look, because he was driving.

"You're right, Benny," said Henry, who was fourteen. "It does look like a dinosaur."

"I *think* it's an old house that's falling

down," said Violet, who was ten.

"Or being mashed by all those green vines that are covering it," Jessie said, who was twelve and often acted motherly toward her younger sister and brother.

"Those green vines are everywhere!" Benny exclaimed. "What are they?"

"The vines are called kudzu," Grandfather Alden told him. "It's considered a weed in the South. People have to fight to keep it from covering everything. I've read it can grow up to four inches a day."

"A monster vine that eats everything," said Jessie.

Benny shivered and pretended to be afraid. He leaned over and said, "Watch, be careful! You don't want to get eaten by the monster vines!"

Watch, a small dog who acted as if he were much bigger, peered out the window and cocked his head. He wasn't sure what Benny was talking about, but he was ready to face it.

Henry, who was sitting in the front seat next to Grandfather, looked up from the map he held. "It looks like we're almost there," he announced. "According to the map, we're only about twelve miles from Elbow Bend, Alabama."

"We are?" Benny asked. "Good. I'm hot. And thirsty!" he said.

"Not hungry, too?" Henry teased Benny.

Benny thought about that for a moment. "Maybe," he said. "I could be hungry, too."

"Don't worry, Benny," Grandfather Alden said. "I'm sure Sally Wade will have a nice cold drink and something waiting for us to eat." Mrs. Sally Wade was an old friend of Grandfather's who had invited the Aldens to visit.

"Oh, good." Benny bounced a little on the seat with excitement. "Then the only other thing we'll need is a good mystery to solve. Let's ask Mrs. Wade if she has a mystery for us when we get there."

"We'll do that," Grandfather agreed. "Although it's a small town, Elbow Bend is famous for its fine old houses. It was one of the first settlements in the state. It's bound to have at least one haunted house."

"Not Mrs. Wade's house?" Benny asked, sounding half afraid and half hopeful.

"No, probably not the Wade house," Grandfather said, smiling.

Benny looked relieved. "Look out, ghosts, here we come!"

With Henry reading the directions, Grandfather had no trouble finding Mrs. Wade's house. Like many of the houses they passed, it was a big old house with a wide front porch. Mrs. Wade's house had a porch upstairs and down and was painted white with dark green shutters. An old oak tree draped with moss shaded the front yard. Flower beds bloomed along the front walk and around the house.

"It doesn't look haunted at all," Benny said. "None of the houses we've passed look haunted."

"Maybe that's a ghost!" said Jessie as the front door of the house opened and a small silver-haired woman stepped out. She shaded her eyes with her hands to see the Aldens better.

Grandfather laughed. "That's no ghost. That's Sally Wade."

Mrs. Wade waved at them. "Y'all are just in time for iced tea and cookies," she called. "Come on in."

Benny and Watch ran up the front walk, while the others followed more slowly.

As Benny got closer, Mrs. Wade smiled. Lines crinkled at the corners of her brown eyes. "I think you must be Benny," she said.

"You're right!" Benny cried. "How did you know? Did Grandfather tell you?"

Before Mrs. Wade could answer, he went on, "And this is Watch. And here comes Jessie — she's twelve — and Violet — she's ten. Henry's fourteen, and we don't know how old Watch is, because we found him. I'm not sure how old Grandfather is, either."

"Old enough," said Grandfather, smiling. He came up the steps and gave Mrs. Wade a hug.

"It's so good to see you, James," Mrs. Wade said. "It's been much too long."

Just then, the door opened and two girls of about eighteen or nineteen came out.

"Hi," said Benny. "Did you bring the cookies?"

The taller of the two girls, who wore her dark brown hair pulled back in a ponytail, said calmly, "Not yet. We'll help you bring your luggage in and show you your rooms first. I'm Kate Frances Wade. Mrs. Wade is my grandmother."

She motioned to the girl next to her, who had curly red hair and green eyes. "And this is Elaine Johnston. She's a real practical joker. You have to keep an eye on her!"

"Call me Lainey," the girl said with a warm smile.

"I'm Benny," Benny said. After everyone had been introduced, Kate Frances and Lainey helped the Aldens bring in their suitcases and showed them to their rooms.

Benny especially liked his room, which was across the hall from Henry's. It was small and fitted neatly under the sloping roof at the back of the house. It had a window with a window seat. Benny and Watch knelt on the pillow there and peered out the window. They saw a big backyard with a garden in it.

"It's nice, Watch. But no boxcar," Benny said.

"Boxcar?" asked Kate Frances, who had taken Benny to his room.

"We have a boxcar in our backyard in Greenfield," Benny explained. "We used to live in it when we were orphans."

"You did?" Kate Frances raised her eyebrows in surprise.

"Yes. Before Grandfather found us and we went to live with him," Benny said.

Henry had come into the room and he and Benny told the story of how the Aldens thought the grandfather they didn't know would be mean so they found the old boxcar in the woods and decided to live there.

"That's where we found Watch," Benny put in.

"Then Grandfather found us," Henry explained. "And we went to live with him."

"And he moved the boxcar. It's behind our house in Greenfield now so we can still

visit it whenever we want," Benny concluded.

"That's quite a story," Kate Frances said. "I'm sorry we don't have a boxcar of our own."

"If you had a ghost, it would be almost as good," Benny said hopefully.

"A ghost? Hmmm. Why don't we go have some tea and cookies," suggested Kate Frances.

They went back downstairs and found Grandfather, Jessie, Violet, and Lainey gathered on the porch. Benny spotted the plate of cookies and the pitcher of iced tea on the porch table.

Lainey poured him a glass of iced tea and he took a cookie and went to sit on the porch swing with Jessie.

"I was talking about our jobs at Elbow Bend State Park," Lainey told them. "Kate Frances and I are working there and staying with Mrs. Wade this summer. We just finished our first year at the state university."

Mrs. Wade pushed open the screen door

and came out with a bowl of water, which she put in the corner of the porch in the shade. "For you, Watch," she said.

Mrs. Wade sat down. Kate Frances poured her some iced tea and said, "Benny's been telling me that he wishes we lived in a haunted house."

"Benny!" said Jessie.

"Well, maybe *next door* to a haunted house," said Benny. "I guess I wouldn't want to live with a ghost."

Everyone laughed, and Benny laughed, too.

"I hate to tell you, Sally," Grandfather said, "but I did say that there *might* be a haunted house in an old town like Elbow Bend."

Mrs. Wade's eyes sparkled. "Now, how did you guess?" she said. "We have a town full of ghosts! And even better, Kate Frances is a very good ghost finder!"

CHAPTER 2

The Ghost Dog of Elbow Bend

"Ghost finder?" Violet's voice squeaked in spite of herself.

"You catch real live ghosts?" Benny asked excitedly.

"But there's no such thing as a ghost. Is there, Grandfather?" Jessie demanded.

"No. Of course not," Grandfather answered.

"I'm not a ghost catcher *or* a ghost finder," Kate Frances said. "I'm a ghost *story* finder."

Henry looked puzzled. "I don't understand," he said.

Kate Frances made a face at her grandmother. Mrs. Wade's eyes crinkled with amusement. "What my grandmother means is that I'm doing research for a special school project on ghost stories. Local ghost stories, to be exact. So I've been interviewing people around Elbow Bend about the ghost stories and tales they grew up hearing."

Lainey said, "After all, just because there is no such thing as a ghost doesn't stop some people from believing the stories, or even thinking they've seen a ghost."

"Are there lots of ghosts in Elbow Bend?" asked Violet, looking around a little nervously.

"They're everywhere," Kate Frances said cheerfully. "It seems like everyone has a story to tell. There's even a famous writer who lives near here who says she has a ghost named Jeffrey living in her house."

"Uh-oh," said Benny.

"But you don't believe in ghosts because

there's no such thing as one, remember, Benny?" Jessie reminded her younger brother.

"Oh, right," said Benny.

"I have an idea," Lainey said. "Now that it's cooling off a little bit, why don't we take a walk?"

The words "take a walk" made Watch raise his head and wag his tail hard.

Lainey went on, "And you can give everyone the ghost-house tour that you gave me when I got here, Kate Frances."

"What a good idea," said Jessie immediately.

Grandfather Alden and Mrs. Wade exchanged glances. "It's still a little hot for me," Grandfather Alden said. "I think I'll stay on the porch a little while longer, and then I'll help Sally start cooking dinner."

"Help is welcome," Mrs. Wade said.

"Okay, then," Henry said. "Let's go!"

Soon the Aldens were walking down the shady streets of the small town. Benny held on to Watch's leash.

Sometimes they would pause and Kate

Frances would tell them stories about the town's houses — and ghosts.

"For example," Kate Frances said, "that house — that's the Pink House." She pointed to a big old house set far back from the sidewalk.

"Is it haunted?" Benny asked.

"Only by the color pink," Lainey told him.

"It's not pink," Jessie objected. "It's just white. With green shutters."

"Ah, but once upon a time, it *was* pink," said Kate Frances, "inside and out. Pink was the owner's favorite color. All the flowers that come up around the house are still pink."

Lainey said, "And they kept one room all pink, too. In honor of the original owner."

Violet rather liked the idea of a house in shades of pink. But since purple was her favorite color, she decided she would prefer a purple house. "Maybe one day I'll live in a purple house," she said aloud.

"With violets all around it," Jessie said.

Violet smiled at the thought.

"Now, there's a house some *do* think is haunted," Kate Frances said as they walked on. This house was smaller, but still big enough to have a wide front porch filled with rocking chairs.

"Is it a good ghost or a bad ghost?" Benny asked.

"A good ghost, I guess," Kate Frances said. "It likes to sit in the rocking chairs on the front porch. People say you can go by on a perfectly still afternoon and one chair will be rocking. Just one."

The Aldens looked at the row of rocking chairs on the front porch. But not one of them moved.

"I guess the ghost isn't out today," Lainey said.

They walked on, up one street and down another. People said hello as they passed and many people knew Kate Frances by name.

"Do you know everybody in Elbow Bend?" Henry asked Kate Frances.

She shook her head. "Not everybody," she said. "But people say hello to everyone

here. They're just friendly, I guess." She smiled and nodded at a woman who was walking by, frowning as she stared at the houses. The woman wore dark glasses, red lipstick, and a big straw hat to protect her from the sun.

"Hello," Kate Frances said.

The woman's dark glasses turned toward Kate Frances. She frowned harder. "Do I know you?" the woman asked.

"No. I was just saying hi," said Kate Frances.

"Oh," said the woman. She turned away and kept walking.

"I guess not *everybody*'s friendly," Henry teased.

Kate Frances laughed. "I guess not," she said.

They paused at a corner while a bus rolled by. People were leaning out the windows of the bus, taking photographs, while a man's voice droned through a loudspeaker inside. Kate Frances nodded toward the bus and added with a mischievous smile, "I don't know all the tourists who come through town."

"How *do* you know so many people?" asked Jessie.

"I've been coming to Elbow Bend every summer since I was a little girl to visit my grandmother, Jessie. That's how I first got interested in ghost stories and folktales, I think. I just loved listening to the grown-ups swap tall tales," Kate Frances said.

"Tall tales?" asked Violet.

"Stories that are just so outrageous they can't be true," said Kate Frances. She stopped. "Now, there's a house with a good tall tale about it."

"Tell it," begged Benny.

"Well, during the full moon in the summer, some say, you can hear the sound of a garden party, right over there behind that wall all covered with jasmine. But if you push open the gate and go inside, the sound stops and nothing is there. Close the gate and come back outside and listen . . . and in a few minutes you'll hear soft laughter and the clinking of glasses."

"Ohhhh," Violet breathed.

"Why? Are they ghosts? Where do they come from?" asked Henry.

"Some people say it's an engagement party for the oldest daughter of the family that lived there long ago. Her fiancé went to war after that and never came back and she died of a broken heart, saying that party was the last happy day she ever had," Kate Frances said, folding her hands over her heart dramatically.

"How sad," said softhearted Violet.

Watch gave a sharp bark.

Lainey looked down and then over at Kate Frances. "Watch says don't forget the ghost dog story."

"Ghost dog? Where does the ghost dog live?" asked Benny.

"Oh, the ghost dog doesn't live anywhere. That's a common ghost story out in the country — here, and in other parts of the world," said Kate Frances. "Sometimes it appears trotting alongside your carriage . . . or these days your car or your bike . . . to warn you of danger.

"The story goes," Kate Frances continued, "that once upon a time, a little dog just showed up in town and made himself at home in the shade of the bench next to the courthouse door. No one knew where he came from or whom he belonged to. He was friendly and several people tried to adopt him, but he wasn't interested. So they fed him and petted him and took care of him as much as he would let them.

"Anyway, he watched the people come and go as if he were waiting for someone, but no one knew who or why. They did know that every once in a while the little dog would stand up and bark — just one sharp bark — at someone who was going into a trial. And when he did, that person was always found guilty. People started calling the little dog 'Judge' and the name stuck.

"Then one day Judge jumped up and started barking like crazy, running around the courthouse and jumping up at the windows. People came running out to see what was wrong, and just about then, the whole building collapsed.

"Well, Judge had saved everyone's life. Somehow, he'd known that building would fall. But when everyone remembered what he'd done and tried to find him to reward him, he was gone. He'd just disappeared. No one ever saw him again. . . .

"Except . . ."

Violet pressed her hands to her cheeks. "Except *when*?" she breathed.

"Except when something terrible is going to happen. Then Judge comes back, waiting and watching and barking and howling to try to warn people. And woe to anyone who doesn't listen to the Ghost Dog of Elbow Bend."

CHAPTER 3

Howls in the Night

Applause broke out.

The Aldens turned in surprise. They had been so interested in the story that Kate Frances was telling, they hadn't even noticed that a small crowd of people had also stopped to listen. Several of them were tourists, with cameras around their necks.

"That was just wonderful," a large man with a big camera said. "May I take your photograph?"

"Sure," said Benny.

"Me, too, me, too," several other people

said. Cameras clicked. One man even had a video camera trained on them. Kate Frances laughed.

"Wasn't that wonderful, Elizabeth?" a young woman said to the older woman standing next to her. It was the woman in the dark glasses, red lipstick, and big hat.

The woman turned up a corner of her mouth. It *might* have been a smile. "I'm hot," she complained. Then, almost reluctantly, she said to Kate Frances, "That wasn't bad. You could almost be a writer."

"Thanks," said Kate Frances as the group began to wander away.

The younger woman smiled. "Elizabeth should know!" she said brightly.

"Come on. Let's get out of the sun," the woman named Elizabeth muttered.

The group on the sidewalk broke up and people drifted away. Henry looked at his wristwatch. "Wow," he said, "almost time for supper."

"We'd better head back," said Kate Frances.

By the time they got back to Mrs. Wade's

house, the evening shadows of the trees had grown long and the sun was almost down. Grandfather Alden was setting the wooden table inside the screened porch.

Soon dinner was on the table and Watch was eating a bowl of dog food nearby.

"Fried chicken," said Grandfather. "If it tastes as good as it smelled while you were cooking it, Sally, it will be delicious."

"It is," mumbled Benny, who'd already reached for a drumstick and taken a big bite.

While they ate, they talked about everything they'd seen that day.

"When I grow up I'm going to have a purple house just like the pink one," Violet said.

"But it won't be just like the pink one if it is purple," Henry teased her gently.

"When I grow up, I'm going to move to Elbow Bend and eat dinner just like this every day," Benny said.

"Well, we don't eat like this every day, Benny," said Mrs. Wade. "But I'm glad you like my cooking." She looked pleased.

Watch finished his meal and walked to

the edge of the porch. He pressed his nose against the screen. He tilted his head as if he were listening to something that no one else could hear.

"This town has lots of stories in it. But no mysteries so far," Jessie said. "Not real mysteries, anyway."

"You like mystery stories?" Lainey asked.

"Oh, yes," said Jessie. "We like to solve them."

"Solve them?" Lainey looked a bit surprised.

"Sure. We've solved lots of mysteries," Henry said. "Even one with a singing ghost."

Kate Frances laughed. "Well, with all the ghost stories people tell around here, maybe a mystery will turn up yet."

Just then, Watch gave one short, sharp bark, then threw back his head and let out a long howl.

Everyone at the table froze.

Then Benny dropped his fork, pushed back his chair, and hurried over to the small dog. "What's wrong, boy?" he asked.

In answer, Watch howled louder.

"Watch?" said Jessie. "Are you okay?"

Then, as quickly as he had begun, Watch stopped howling. But the fur on his back stayed up and he kept his nose pressed against the screen for a long moment.

Benny wrapped his arms around Watch's neck. Watch turned his head and licked Benny's cheek.

Looking up at everyone at the table, Benny said, "I know what Watch saw. He saw the ghost dog!"

"Benny! You know there is no such thing as a ghost. Or a ghost dog," Jessie said.

Violet didn't say anything. She stared out at the darkness and the fireflies, half expecting to see a ghost dog float by.

"Watch could have been howling at anything," Henry said. "An owl hooting that we couldn't hear. Or a siren far away."

"Come have dessert, Benny," Grandfather said. "I'm sure the reason Watch howled is as simple as a hooting owl. No ghosts."

Benny looked through the screen at the

night, but he didn't see anything. Whatever had caused Watch to howl had stopped — or gone away.

Later that night Benny and Watch came into Henry's room. Benny, who was wearing his pajamas, rubbed his eyes and yawned. Henry looked up from his book.

Benny said, "Watch and I came to say good night."

"Good night," said Henry. "And remember, I'm just across the hall if you get scared or anything."

"Scared?" Benny said. "I'm never scared. Only, maybe, a little worried sometimes."

Henry smiled at his younger brother. "Well, if you get a little worried, just call me. I'll be right here."

"Okay," said Benny. "And if you're worried about the ghost dog, don't be. Watch will protect us."

"There isn't a ghost dog, Benny. That's just a story," Henry said.

Benny looked as if he might want to argue with Henry. But all he said was, "Good night."

"Good night," said Henry.

When Benny stepped into the hall, he saw Lainey, who motioned for him to follow her. "Come on," she said. "We'll help the ghost dog pay Henry a visit."

"How?" asked Benny.

"With an old Halloween mask I found in the closet in my room. It's a basset hound mask."

"You mean, play a joke on him?" ask Benny.

"Yep," said Lainey.

A few minutes later, wearing the dog mask, Benny walked back down the hall. When he reached the door, Lainey turned off the hall light.

No light showed under Henry's door. Benny wondered if his older brother was already asleep.

If he was, Benny and Lainey were about to awaken him!

"Scratch on the door a little, like a dog, but softly," Lainey told Benny.

Benny scratched on a lower panel of

the door. As he did, Lainey let out a soft moan.

Benny thought he heard a sound from Henry's room.

He scratched again. Lainey let out a low howl that sounded pretty scary to Benny.

"What? Who's there?" Henry's voice sounded as if he had been asleep.

Lainey howled once more.

The light in Henry's room came on. He threw open the door. Lainey howled again, and Benny did, too.

Henry jumped back. Then he realized who it was.

"Benny! Lainey!" he exclaimed.

"No, it's the ghost dog," said Lainey, turning on the hall light. She and Benny began to laugh.

Henry shook his head, grinning. "You almost fooled me. Almost."

Benny threw his arms around his brother. "Good night," he said again. "We promise not to let the ghost dog wake you up anymore!"

Henry rolled his eyes. "I'll count on it. Good night."

"That was a pretty good joke," Benny said.

He went into his room and got into bed. Benny put his flashlight by his bed, just in case, then turned out the light and pulled the sheet up to his chin. He stared at the darkness. Was that a ghostly white shape by the window?

He clicked on the flashlight.

No, it was just a vase of white flowers.

Benny yawned. A moment later he was sound asleep.

Violet blinked and sat up in her bed. What had awakened her?

She glanced at the clock by her bed. It was midnight, exactly.

Just as she realized how late it was, Violet heard a low-sounding howl float through her open window. And then another. And another.

The ghost dog, Violet thought and grabbed the covers to pull them up around her.

Then another howl, much closer, made her gasp.

It was coming from inside the house!

Violet dropped the covers, grabbed for her robe, and ran out of her room. She just missed crashing into Jessie, who was running out of her room, too.

They heard the howl again.

"Benny's room," Jessie cried. "Hurry!"

Henry bolted out of his room and joined them. He threw open the door of Benny's room and switched on the light.

Benny was kneeling at the window seat, holding Watch's collar. He turned toward them. "The ghost dog!" he cried. "It's here!"

Just then, Watch threw back his head and let out another long howl. It made the hair on Violet's neck stand up, almost like the hair on Watch's neck.

More howls from nearby yards and houses joined Watch's.

And then, just as suddenly as it had begun, the howling died away.

Now the night was perfectly still. Not even the crickets sang.

"Watch, are you okay? What's wrong, boy?" Jessie asked. She went to Watch and patted his head.

Watch didn't seem to notice. He just peered out through the window screen into the night.

"What's going on?" It was Kate Frances, with Lainey behind her. They stood in Benny's doorway.

Benny turned to face everyone. "It was the ghost dog," he said. "It was calling Watch and all the other dogs, too."

"What? That's impossible!" Kate Frances said.

"I *thought* I heard dogs howling," Lainey said.

But Jessie said, "Real dogs, Benny. Only real dogs were howling. In the first place, there's no such thing as a ghost."

"It was probably an animal of some kind he heard," Kate Frances said. "Just like he did during dinner this evening. Maybe a raccoon or a fox is living in the strip of woods along the creek that runs across the bottom of the backyard."

"If it was just an animal, Watch would have barked, not howled," Benny said.

"It's nothing to worry about, Benny," Henry assured him. "Why, Grandfather and Mrs. Wade slept right through it. If it hadn't been for Watch, we probably would have, too."

Benny sighed.

"Let's get some sleep," Henry said. "We've got a big day tomorrow."

Kate Frances was frowning. But she said, "Right. Y'all are going to Elbow Bend State Park with Lainey and me tomorrow."

When everyone had left and the room was dark and quiet again, Benny whispered to Watch, "If you see the ghost dog again, Watch, just howl. And we'll catch it!"

CHAPTER 4

Clues in the Park

But Watch didn't howl anymore that night and when Benny woke up, sunlight was pouring in through the window. He jumped out of bed and got dressed as quickly as he could.

As he and Watch hurried down the stairs, his nose told him that someone had already made biscuits. He joined everyone else in the kitchen for a breakfast of buttered biscuits with blackberry jam, along with grits and ham. Even Watch got a piece of ham.

Grandfather said to Benny, "I hear Watch

did some midnight singing last night."

"He howled," Benny agreed.

"I understand Watch wasn't the only dog in town who howled at midnight," Mrs. Wade said.

"Something made Watch and all the other dogs howl last night," Benny said.

Jessie shook her head. But she only said, "I think I'm going to have another biscuit."

"Me, too," said Violet. "They are delicious."

"When we're finished with breakfast, it'll be time to go to work," Kate Frances said.

"Are we going to work with you?" Violet asked.

Kate Frances smiled. "Maybe we can find a job for you, if you want one."

Elbow Bend State Park was by a big curve in the river. Kate Frances drove past a small ticket booth and waved at the older man inside, who was wearing an ELBOW BEND STAFF cap. She parked the car in a small parking lot behind a building made of rough-cut wood and led the way inside.

"Good morning, Kate Frances. Good

morning, Lainey." A woman came out of a small office right by the front door.

"Good morning, Ms. Hedge," said Kate Frances. "I've brought some volunteers for the day." She introduced the four Aldens.

"We have plenty of work for you. We need someone to stack all the pamphlets in our information booths and to help hand out maps."

"I can do that," Violet said.

"Me, too," said Benny.

Ms. Hedge said, "Kate Frances, I'm counting on you to help me plan the Stories Under the Stars program. It's only two days away, you know."

"Stories Under the Stars?" asked Henry.

Ms. Hedge nodded. "Yes. There is a storyteller who lives near here. She's a well-known storyteller and she'll be here tomorrow night at our outdoor theater. You should come. She's wonderful."

"We will," said Jessie.

"We can sit in the employee section," Kate Frances said. "My grandmother was already planning on coming and I know your grandfather would enjoy it, too."

"Good," said Ms. Hedge. She turned to Lainey and continued, "The ground crew needs a little help today, Lainey, if you don't mind pitching in. Someone knocked over all the litter containers on Bluff Trail and Overlook Trail."

"Good grief," said Lainey. "Who'd do a thing like that?"

"Maybe it was a wild animal," said Violet. "A raccoon. Or a bear."

"No bears around here," Ms. Hedge said, to Violet's secret relief. "And I doubt a raccoon is strong enough to turn over those big containers." Her lips tightened a little. "No, it was someone's stupid idea of a joke."

"Well, let's get to work," said Lainey. "Henry, Jessie, you want to come along?"

"Sure," said Jessie.

"And we can look for clues," Henry added. "Maybe we can solve the Mystery of the Garbage Can Litterbug."

Lainey laughed. "Maybe. Let's get packs from the equipment room and some sandwiches. We'll have a picnic lunch on the trail."

Kate Frances said, "And we'll have a picnic right here."

"See you this afternoon," Violet said. She and Benny went to work in the visitors' center while Henry and Jessie set out on the trails with Lainey.

"Wow," Jessie said as she stuffed newspaper into the litter sack slung over one shoulder. "Some people sure are litterbugs."

It was hot, hard work. Henry and Jessie looked for clues that might help them figure out who would upend all the litter cans — or why. But there were too many footprints on the trail to point to any one suspect and they could find nothing else that helped.

"Whew! That's done. Let's head back," Lainey said at last. "I just hope whoever pulled the trash can tricks doesn't come back."

"Me, too," said Henry.

As they came out of the woods into the main clearing of the park, Henry said, "What's that old cabin over there?"

"Oh. That's one of the cabins of the original European settlers here," Lainey said. "Or what's left of it. In this corner of the park and back through the woods are what's left of several houses of the people who used to live here over two hundred years ago. Dr. Sage sometimes camps out here. She's the archaeologist in charge of digging up the historic sites in the park. Why don't we go meet her?"

As Lainey, Henry, and Jessie approached the old ruined cabin, a woman peered from around the back of the house. "Stay between the ropes," she barked. "Or you'll be trampling on history."

Henry and Jessie were a little startled by this sharp welcome, but Lainey seemed used to it. "Hi, Dr. Sage," she said. "It's just me. I brought some friends to meet you. This is Henry and Jessie. They're staying with Mrs. Wade and doing some volunteer work in the park."

Dr. Sage came out from around the corner of the house. She was a small, strong-looking woman, with dark skin. Her dark brown eyes seemed to miss nothing. She wiped one hand on the leg of her dirt-smudged jeans and said, "Hello."

Jessie and Henry said hello and shook hands.

"So you're volunteering. That's good. Saves the park money. Money saved is money I can use to do my digging and research," Dr. Sage said.

"I'm glad," Jessie replied politely.

Dr. Sage gave a short laugh. "Just don't mess with anything around our dig. It may look untidy, but we can tell when someone's been here who shouldn't have been. People on the tour groups have actually tried to pick up artifacts to take home!"

Jessie and Henry both were about to protest that they knew better than to touch historic ruins uninvited, but Dr. Sage stopped them by raising her voice and shouting, "Brad! You've got company!"

"Coming," a voice called from the edge

of the nearby trees. A few seconds later a tall, lanky young man with long hair pulled back in a short ponytail came ambling out of the woods. Although it didn't seem possible, he was covered with even more smudges of dirt than Dr. Sage.

"Lainey's here to say hello to you," Dr. Sage said.

"And to introduce some volunteers," Lainey said quickly. Henry noticed that Lainey was blushing. When he looked over at Brad, he thought Brad's cheeks were red, too, but it might have been sunburn.

Brad smiled and shook hands with the Aldens. "Hi, I'm Brad Thompson."

"Are you finding anything interesting?" Henry asked Brad after they'd been introduced.

"As a matter of fact, I've found some very interesting pottery fragments," Brad said. "It leads me to believe that I'm on the right track to the town dump."

"Dump?" ask Jessie, thinking of all the garbage and litter they'd just picked up along the trail.

Brad nodded eagerly. "Yes! Isn't it great news?"

Seeing their puzzled looks, Dr. Sage explained, "If we study what people of earlier times threw away, it can tell us quite a lot."

Jessie laughed. "Wait until we tell Benny that the scientists here are studying *garbage*, especially after we cleaned it up all day."

Lainey shook her head and smiled. "I guess we should go and let you get back to work."

"Good idea," Henry agreed.

They all said good-bye to Dr. Sage and Brad. Brad looked up and said, " 'Bye, Lainey, and, uh . . . everyone."

Dr. Sage didn't even notice that they were leaving.

"Are they always like that?" Henry asked.

"Worse," said Lainey with a little sigh. "Brad and Dr. Sage would work all day and all night if they could. They'd be happy if we closed this park to everyone but scientists and historians."

"But you're practically a historian, aren't you?" Jessie asked.

"I'll be a historian when I finish college. Right now I'm just a history student," Lainey said, with one last glance back at Brad.

"Look," said Jessie. "There's Violet outside the visitors' center."

"And Benny, too," Henry said.

Violet had a map in her hand and was pointing to it while she talked to an attractive woman with sleek black hair. The woman had on tiny square-framed sunglasses and bright red lipstick.

Violet then gave the map to the pretty tourist, who stuffed it into a pocket and walked away.

Benny and Violet hurried over to join Henry, Jessie, and Lainey.

"We've given out about a million maps," Benny said.

No one got a chance to answer because just then an angry voice shouted, "Hey! Stay on the paths, like you're supposed to!"

A tall, strongly built man in work pants, work boots, and a long-sleeved shirt that said ELBOW BEND STAFF stomped up to them. He had a rake in one hand, which he waved. "Can't you read?" he demanded. "What does that sign say?" He gestured toward a small green-and-white sign at the base of a tree.

" 'Please stay on the . . . trails,' " Benny read aloud.

"And where are you standing?" the man growled.

Benny looked down at his feet. He looked over at Violet. "I guess we kind of took a shortcut *between* the trails," he said.

"Huh," said the man. "First you walk right through the leaves I've raked up. Then you go and knock over all my garbage cans. Tourists!"

"We work here," Violet said, finding her voice.

"And we didn't knock over anything," added Benny.

The man stepped back, pushed up his cap, and studied them.

Just then Kate Frances came up the trail. She said, "It's true. These are friends of mine and they're doing some volunteer work."

"Well," the man said grudgingly, "I guess you're not tourists. I guess you're not *so* bad. I'm Joshua Wilson, head of the grounds crew. You can call me Joshua. That's good enough for me."

He paused. "But you still have to obey the rules." He stalked off, waving his rake and muttering to himself.

"Wow. He's grumpy," said Jessie.

"He's proud of this park. It upsets him when people don't treat it right. And you can't blame him for being grumpy after someone knocked over all the garbage containers," Kate Frances told them. "Joshua thinks we should limit the number of tourists allowed in here. He says it would be better for the park."

"Did you find any clues?" Benny asked, turning to Henry and Jessie, just remembering the garbage can mystery.

Henry shook his head.

"Not a single one," Jessie said.

Then Benny remembered another mystery. "Hey, Kate Frances," he said as they walked toward the car to drive home for the evening. "Are there any ghosts in Elbow Bend State Park?"

"Nope," said Kate Frances. "Not even a ghost dog."

But as it turned out, Kate Frances was wrong.

CHAPTER 5

Tourists Keep Out?

The next morning, as the Aldens walked toward the Elbow Bend State Park visitors' center, they saw Dr. Sage and Brad. Henry and Jessie had told Violet and Benny about the scientist, and Lainey and Kate Frances had promised to introduce them.

But the two girls didn't get a chance.

Dr. Sage turned toward them as they came up, put her hands on her hips, and said, "You children didn't do any volunteer digging last night, did you?"

"No!" said Henry.

"Why? What's wrong?" Lainey asked.

"Someone's been at the site. Whoever it was made several holes. We just reported it," Brad said.

"May we see?" asked Jessie.

"I guess so," Dr. Sage agreed. "Come on."

When everyone reached the site, Dr. Sage led the way on a worn footpath lined by vivid yellow nylon cord strung between metal stakes. Signs taped to the cord said, OFFICIAL STATE HISTORIC SITE and KEEP OFF.

Brad said, "Over here." He stepped over the cord and raised it up so that the others could duck under. Walking carefully around the edge of a shallow rectangle in the earth, Brad pointed.

Next to the rectangle was a deep hole, with dirt flung up messily all around it.

Benny squatted down next to the hole. "Wow," he said. "It looks just like the holes Watch digs. Only bigger."

"It's no dog or wild animal," Dr. Sage

said. "That's not typical behavior for a dog — to go around digging holes all over the place like this."

"And in just one night," said Brad. "Plus, there are no dog or fox footprints. No animal tracks of any kind."

"Did anything get stolen?" Violet asked as they walked from one place to another, examining all the holes.

"No," said Brad. "In fact, I found several pieces of pottery at one of the sites, scattered around with the dirt that had been scooped out."

"Look at this," Benny said as they reached the last hole, on the edge of the site. "It's a *bone!*"

Everyone peered over Benny's shoulder into the bucket-sized hole in the red dirt. Brad leaned down and picked up the small white object.

Brad sniffed the bone. "It's a chicken bone. From a fried chicken dinner, unless I'm mistaken. But what's it doing way out here?"

"I know," said Benny. He looked around

at the others, his eyes wide. "It's the ghost dog! It was burying a bone — but then morning came and scared it away!"

"Ghost dog?" Dr. Sage's features seemed to grow sharper. "Not at my dig!"

"I know that old ghost dog story," Brad said. He smiled. "I don't think it was a ghost dog, Benny. I think someone is playing a stupid joke."

"If I catch who did it, I'll make them sorry they ever thought of doing something like this," growled Dr. Sage. She looked at Brad. "Let's get to work. We'll leave the holes. No use disturbing the site even more."

"We need to get to work, too," Kate Frances agreed.

They all headed back to the visitors' center.

"That's the second time in two days that something weird has happened in the park," noted Henry. "First the garbage getting dumped all over the trails. Then all those holes."

"It does sound a little like something a dog would do, doesn't it?" Jessie said.

"But it's not," Violet said. "It's definitely a person."

"The park is locked at night, or at least the entrance gate is," Kate Frances said. "Whoever did it would have had to sneak in here at night, and there would be . . ."

"Snakes." Lainey shuddered. "They come out at night. I'm afraid of them. We *do* have rattlesnakes around here."

"Not many," said Kate Frances. "And besides, they're more afraid of you than you are of them. They won't hurt you unless you try to hurt them."

"Huh," said Lainey. "I don't want to try to hurt a snake. I don't even want to go *near* one."

They all thought hard for a moment. Then Jessie said, "Maybe someone is mad at the park. Have you fired anyone lately?"

"No," said Kate Frances. "Everyone has worked here for years, except for the summer students, like Lainey and me."

"Maybe it's one of the tourists," said Henry.

"But why?" asked Lainey.

"You could ask Joshua that," suggested Violet. "He thinks tourists are annoying, remember? He would believe they'd turn over trash cans and dig holes in the middle of the night."

"Yes . . . or maybe Joshua is doing it to make it look like the tourists did it," Henry said.

Lainey looked puzzled. "I don't get it," she said.

"To get the park to limit the number of tourists," Jessie said.

Kate Frances shook her head. "It's an interesting idea, but I don't think Joshua would do that. I just can't see him sneaking around in the middle of the night, for one thing."

"Well," said Jessie, "somebody's doing it."

"Or some *ghost*," Benny said under his breath.

"So it looks like we have a mystery to solve after all," Jessie concluded.

* * *

No dogs howled that night. Benny and Watch and everyone else in Mrs. Wade's house slept without being awakened until the sun came up the next morning.

But when they got to the park, they found Ms. Hedge talking to Dr. Sage.

"Dr. Sage looks really unhappy," said Violet softly in Jessie's ear.

Although Violet hadn't meant for Dr. Sage to hear, she did. She turned, folded her arms, and narrowed her eyes at the Aldens. "Dr. Sage *is* unhappy," she stated.

She turned back to Ms. Hedge. "Well. Do we get a night guard? Some kind of security?"

"I'm afraid we can't afford that right now," Ms. Hedge said. "We — "

Dr. Sage snorted. "Figures," she said. Without waiting for Ms. Hedge to reply, Dr. Sage turned and walked away.

The Aldens promptly followed.

"What's wrong?" Henry asked the archaeologist.

"Holes," she said. She was walking so fast

that the Aldens almost had to run to keep up.

"More holes at the site?" asked Jessie, panting a little.

"No. Different holes," Dr. Sage answered.

"What do you mean?" said Benny.

She didn't reply but just kept walking.

And since she didn't object, the Aldens stayed with her. When they reached the site, Dr. Sage led them straight back to where the first hole had been. Brad was squatting by the dig, sifting dirt through what appeared to be a large strainer.

"The detectives are back," said Dr. Sage.

Brad looked up. "Oh," he said. "Uh, did Lainey come with you?"

"Just us," said Benny.

"Well, take a look," said Dr. Sage.

The Aldens went into the roped-off area. The holes from the day before had been filled in, more or less — but other holes had been dug nearby.

"Take a look around," Dr. Sage said. "But watch where you put your feet. Just because someone is dancing around here at night digging holes doesn't mean you can trample over our hard work."

She stalked away.

"Did you find any clues?" Henry asked Brad.

Brad shook his head. "No. Nothing. Not even a chicken bone this time."

The Aldens examined each new hole carefully. All of the original holes had been filled in with dirt. Now there were brand-new holes!

"Why would someone do all this?" Violet wondered.

"Maybe they're looking for something," said Jessie.

Benny saw something in the dirt. He leaned down and gingerly picked up a small scrap of leather. He held it up. It was twisted and covered with dirt. But even so, he knew what it was.

"Look!" he cried. "A dog collar!"

"A dog collar!" exclaimed Violet. "What's a dog collar doing here?"

Brad looked surprised at Benny's find.

"Wow," he said. "If it's real, it'll be a great little piece of history. This is the sort of thing that you put on display for tourists, you know? Perfect for the kind of exhibits they'd pay to see. . . ."

"Is it a really old collar?" asked Henry.

"Hard to say," Brad mused. "Not very much of it left. It's worn. But it's in very good condition for something that would have to have been in the ground for over a hundred years. If it still had any metalwork on it, I could tell right away. They made dog collars by hand back then."

He stood up. "Thanks," he said to Benny, and wandered away toward the small trailer pulled up nearby, where Dr. Sage was reading on the steps.

"I found a clue," Benny said triumphantly.

"You did," agreed Henry. "And maybe two other suspects."

"What do you mean?" Violet asked.

"I know," said Jessie. "You mean that maybe Dr. Sage and Brad dug those holes."

"That's right. To get some publicity. And

maybe to force whoever's in charge to give them some more money for their research," Henry said.

"And I've thought of one more," Jessie said.

"Who?" asked Benny. "Did I find that clue, too?"

"Sorry, no, Benny," Jessie told him. "It's Lainey. I think we have to add her to our list of suspects."

"Lainey!" exclaimed Violet. "Oh, no."

But Henry was nodding. "Because she likes to play jokes, like that joke about the ghost dog she played on me with Benny."

"That's right," agreed Jessie. "Lainey could be doing all of this as a practical joke, a sort of challenge to us as detectives."

Violet said reluctantly, "I guess she could. She *was* awfully interested in the stories about solving mysteries that we told her at dinner our first night here."

"It could even be Lainey *and* Brad," Henry mused. "After all, they seem to like each other."

"They do seem to like each other," said Jessie. "If Lainey thought it would help Brad's work at the dig, she might help him dig holes to get extra publicity."

"Or even to help Dr. Sage!" added Benny.

Holding up her hand, Violet said, "So we have how many suspects? One: Joshua, the head of the grounds crew. Two: Dr. Sage. Three: Lainey. Four: Brad."

"We have a lot more suspects than clues," said Jessie.

"That's happened before," Henry said. "Don't worry. We'll solve this mystery."

"Meanwhile," Jessie said, "let's get to work. And everybody, be sure and keep your eyes and ears open for more clues. You never know when one will turn up!"

Although the Aldens did just what Jessie had suggested, they found no more clues. It was hot outdoors and lots of tourists were visiting the park. As the day was ending, even more began to show up.

"They're here for the storytelling hour,"

Henry said. "It's a good thing we have special reserved seats."

"Grandfather and Mrs. Wade will be here soon, too," said Benny. "I hope they don't forget our picnic dinner."

"They won't, Benny. Don't worry," Violet reassured him.

Just then they passed Joshua Wilson, who was pushing a wheelbarrow toward the tool and gardening shed.

"Good evening, Joshua," said Jessie.

He looked up. Then he looked over at the people following the signs that said, STORIES UNDER THE STARS. He shook his head. "This place will be a mess tomorrow," he said. "Trampled. Full of garbage. Storytelling. Bah!" He pushed the wheelbarrow away to the shed and put it away, still grumbling.

Benny said, "Look. There's Grandfather."

The Aldens hurried to join Grandfather Alden and Mrs. Wade as they made their way toward the outdoor theater. The trail wound through the woods and stopped at a small clearing. In it stood a small wooden stage beneath a curved roof that looked like a large half clamshell. Facing the stage were rows of wooden benches.

Kate Frances waved at them and they made their way to a section of seats near the front. "Here we go," she said. "Just in time for dinner and storytelling."

"Where's Lainey?" asked Henry.

"She's up at the parking lot, directing people," Mrs. Wade answered. "She'll join us if she can."

Henry nodded.

They ate dinner and watched as more and more people arrived. Some had brought picnic dinners, too. As it grew later and darker, soft lights began to shine around the edges of the theater.

Then all the lights went dark for a moment. When they came back on, a hush had fallen over the audience. Spotlighted on the stage was a small woman dressed in a bonnet and old-fashioned clothes.

People applauded and cheered. And then

everyone grew still so that the only sounds were the wind in the trees and the voice of the storyteller.

It had grown late and the storyteller was just finishing when a mournful howl filled the night.

The storyteller stopped. Everyone froze.

Benny grabbed Violet's arm. "The ghost dog!" he cried.

No sooner had he spoken than someone screamed. A man jumped to his feet and pointed. "A ghost. It's a ghost!" he shouted.

CHAPTER 6

No Footprints

Some people jumped up to look.

But most of the audience just stared as a small white doglike figure seemed to float through the dark shadows beneath the huge old trees at the far side of the clearing.

And then it was gone.

"Everyone stay calm," said the storyteller. She raised her hands. "I'm glad you enjoyed the conclusion of our performance."

"Oh, it was part of the act," a man near the Aldens said in a relieved voice.

"I knew it wasn't a real dog," said a freckle-faced girl with wiry red hair.

An older woman began to applaud and the rest of the crowd did, too.

Benny, who had jumped up on the bench to see better, turned to Kate Frances. "It was part of the show?" he asked in a disappointed voice.

Kate Frances made a face. "If it was," she said, "no one told me about it."

"So it was real?" Violet gasped.

"I don't know *what* it was," she said. "But as soon as we have seen to it that all the guests have gone, I'm going to find out."

Henry turned to Grandfather Alden. "We need to look into this," he said. "We can get a ride back to Mrs. Wade's house with Kate Frances."

"That'll be fine," said Grandfather, his eyes twinkling.

"Good luck looking for clues," Mrs. Wade added.

"Let's go look for footprints," Jessie said. "A ghost doesn't leave footprints."

They turned to walk to the dark trees at

the edge of the clearing. Henry said, "Violet? Are you coming?"

Violet was looking up at the stage, where Kate Frances was talking to the storyteller. Lainey had joined them, as had several other people. They were all talking and several were holding out pens and paper for an autograph. Violet stared at one of the people in the group who seemed familiar somehow. . . .

"Violet?" Henry said again.

"I remember now!" Violet said suddenly. "I remember where I've seen that woman!"

"Which one?" asked Benny.

"The one with the black hair and the red lipstick. I'm sure it's her," Violet said.

Benny, Jessie, and Henry studied the dark-haired woman. She was talking and waving her hands at the storyteller onstage. Then she held out a book and flipped open the pages.

Jessie said, "Oh. I remember her, too. She was one of the tourists who took Kate Frances's photograph the first day we were here."

"Well, it's too bad she didn't take a picture of the ghost dog," Benny said. He paused, then added, "Of course, you can't really take a picture of a ghost."

"True. But you can look for footprints," said Henry. "Let's go."

But although the Aldens searched all along the edge of the clearing, kneeling on the ground to brush away leaves and covering every inch of ground where the ghost dog had been, they didn't find anything that would help them solve the mystery.

They didn't find a single paw print.

"There *was* a dog," Violet said. "We all saw it!"

"A glowing dog that floated along the ground and didn't leave any footprints," said Henry.

"And we heard it howl," Jessie said. She stopped, frowned, and said, "No, we didn't. The howling happened just *as* the dog was floating by here. But it seemed to be coming from somewhere else."

"Another dog was howling?" asked

Benny. "Well, it wasn't Watch. He's at Mrs. Wade's. If he was howling, we couldn't have heard him."

"Hey! Time to go!" they heard Kate Frances call. She pointed in the direction of the car and then she, Lainey, and the storyteller began to walk up the path.

The Aldens followed. They talked about the case as they walked.

Jessie said, "We've heard dogs howling in town. And now we saw a ghost dog here and heard a dog howling," she went on.

"And someone, or something, is digging holes where Dr. Sage and Brad are working," Violet said.

"Someone has also tipped over garbage cans along trails," Jessie said. "So it looks as if someone is working against the Elbow Bend State Park."

"What's that got to do with a ghost dog howling in town at midnight?" Benny asked.

"Maybe nothing. Maybe that isn't part of the mystery, Benny. Maybe it's just a coincidence," Violet said. "And maybe there's no ghost dog in the town of Elbow Bend. After all, we haven't seen one there."

Ahead of them, the others reached the parking lot.

"Look, there's Joshua," said Henry.

They watched as the grounds-crew chief picked up a piece of paper and put it into a nearby trash can, with a glare at the remaining people. He opened the passenger door of a station wagon and they saw another groundskeeper driving. "Thanks for the ride," they heard Joshua say. "I don't know when that car of mine will be fixed."

Joshua slammed the door and the car drove away. Then the storyteller got into her car and drove away, too. Now only Lainey and Kate Frances and a few of the audience members were left.

"There *is* a ghost dog in Elbow Bend," Benny insisted. "Even if we haven't seen it, we've heard it!"

They'd reached the parking lot now, and everyone heard Benny's words. Faces turned in their direction.

"Ghost dog in Elbow Bend?" the woman with the dark hair cried. "Did you say you'd seen it there?"

"No. I've just heard it. I only saw it tonight," Benny said.

Some people stopped walking and turned to listen. The woman turned to Kate Frances and Lainey and said in a loud voice, "See? I knew it wasn't part of the show. I knew the ghost dog was real! And you owe it to the public to tell the truth about what's going on in this town, as well as everything that's happened in this park!"

The woman looked from Kate Frances to Lainey. Kate Frances just shook her head. "There is no such thing as a ghost," she said. "There's a logical explanation for all of this, and we don't need to frighten people with old ghost stories."

"You have to tell people the truth," said the woman, and marched away across the parking lot and down the road.

Kate Frances said, "Great. Why is this happening all of a sudden? I think she's some kind of writer. Probably a reporter.

This'll probably turn up in the news."

Brad, who was standing by Lainey, said, "Too bad Dr. Sage was at that dinner party. She'd have been very interested in all of this."

"Well, don't worry," Lainey said to Kate Frances. "We'll just pretend none of this happened."

"Yes," said Kate Frances. "But somehow, I don't think ignoring it is going to make our troubles go away."

"OOOOooooohhhh! OOOOooooohhh!" Loud howls sounded in the night.

Benny sat up. He grabbed for the lamp on the bedside table and flicked the switch. Light flooded his bedroom as Watch answered the ghostly noise with a howl of his own.

The door opened and Henry came in. "Are you okay, Benny?"

Before Benny could answer, more howls rose up from all around the neighborhood. Dogs all over Elbow Bend were joining in the ghostly chorus.

"Twelve midnight exactly," Jessie said, coming in behind Henry, with Violet on her heels.

Suddenly Watch flattened his ears and barked.

Benny ran to the screen and tried to see out.

"Turn out the light," Henry said. "We can see out better without it."

Violet switched off the light.

Almost at once Watch barked again, a short warning bark. At the same time, Benny cried, "There it is! The ghost dog!"

The Aldens crowded around the window. Sure enough, at the foot of the lawn, a small white figure was floating along the ground, rising and falling.

"Come on! We can catch that dog!" Jessie said. She turned and ran out of the room.

"Get your flashlight, Benny," Henry said. "Let's go."

The Aldens thundered down the stairs of the old house, through the hall, and out the kitchen door into the backyard.

Behind them, they heard Grandfather call, "What's wrong?"

"The ghost dog!" Benny called over his shoulder.

With their flashlights crisscrossing the night, they ran across the long sloping lawn.

The dog was nowhere to be seen.

Watch barked again and raced into the woods.

"Watch! Wait for us!" Benny called. He ran after the small, brave dog, wondering what he would do if he and Watch actually caught the ghost.

They thrashed through the trees, ran through the backyard of another house, and came out on a street. Watch stood under a dim streetlight, staring up the road. He was growling in a soft disapproving way when the Aldens reached him.

"Did you see the ghost?" Benny asked. He dropped to his knees and hugged Watch. "Good dog!"

Violet said, "Why would a ghost run out to a street and then disappear?"

"I have a better question," said Jessie.

"How could Watch smell a ghost to track it this far? Only a *real* dog would have a smell!"

"The howling has stopped," Violet said. "Listen."

It was true. Now the night sounds of crickets and the wind in the trees were all they could hear.

"I guess we'd better get back," Henry said. "But this time, we'll use the street instead of cutting through someone's backyard!"

As they walked back, Jessie said, "It's definite. The ghost dog is part of the mystery at Elbow Bend State Park."

"Trash cans tipped over, holes dug, dogs howling, and a glowing white dog that doesn't leave footprints." Violet reeled off the list of events.

"It doesn't make sense," Henry said. "Why would the dog appear at the park, and here, in town, in our backyard?"

They'd almost reached the house when Jessie stopped. "Let's go take another look in the woods," she said. "I have an idea. But first . . ." Untying her bathrobe, she took the sash and looped it through Watch's collar.

"What're you doing that for?" asked Violet.

"You'll see," said Jessie mysteriously.

Once more, but at a slower pace, Jessie led the way across Mrs. Wade's big backyard on the trail of the ghost dog. "Here, Watch," she said when they'd reached the trees at the foot of the yard. "Find the dog. Find the dog."

Watch immediately began to tug on the sash. He pulled Jessie along through the woods, his nose to the ground. He zigzagged in and out among trees and through bushes.

Suddenly Jessie hauled back on the makeshift leash. "Whoa, Watch," she said. Turning her flashlight slightly to one side of where Watch stood expectantly, she said, "There. See it?"

"It . . . glows," Violet said.

"What is it?" Benny asked.

Henry bent over the dash of white on the

rough trunk of a tree. He touched it and pulled back a finger. "It's wet," he said.

"It's paint," said Jessie.

"Glow-in-the-dark paint!" Violet explained.

"That's why we saw a dog that glowed in the dark," Jessie said. "Someone had put paint on part of its coat."

"It's not a ghost?" Benny asked.

"Not at all. This is proof," Henry answered, holding up his paint-dotted fingertip.

"But how could whoever did this make the dog float?" Violet asked. "And why? And why dig the holes and turn over the trash cans? Why would they want everyone to believe that a ghost dog is haunting Elbow Bend?"

"I don't know," said Henry.

The Aldens began to walk back toward the house.

"It could be Joshua, trying to scare tourists away from Elbow Bend," said Jessie. "He was at the storytelling session, but we didn't see him when the ghost dog appeared. And it would be easy for him to sneak into the park and turn over trash cans and dig holes."

"Yes. He's a very good suspect. But it does seem as if the appearance of a ghost dog would bring more tourists, rather than fewer," mused Henry.

"Maybe." Jessie thought for a moment. "And don't forget Joshua's car is broken. He couldn't drive here in the middle of the night without a car that worked."

"Unless someone was helping him," said Violet.

"Maybe . . . but what about Lainey? She could be playing a practical joke."

"Yes. We didn't see her tonight at all, until after the ghost dog had come and gone," agreed Violet reluctantly. She didn't want it to be Lainey. She liked her.

"Or Dr. Sage, to raise money for the park and her digging project," Henry said. "She wasn't even at the storytelling session. But maybe she didn't come so she could sneak up and make us believe we'd seen — and heard — a ghost dog."

"Don't forget Brad," Benny said. "He was there, too."

"Yes. But again, we didn't see him until after the ghost dog had appeared and then disappeared," Violet said. "He could be helping Dr. Sage — or Lainey."

"We have lots of suspects," Benny said. "How do we pick out the person who did it?"

"That's the mystery, Benny," said Henry. "And I'm not sure how we're going to solve it."

CHAPTER 7

An Exciting Discovery

"I don't have to work at the park this morning, so I'm going to walk to town to do a little shopping," Lainey said the next morning after breakfast. "Who wants to come with me?"

"I do," said Benny.

"Me, too," echoed Jessie and Violet.

"Count me in," Henry said.

"And I've got to get to work," said Kate Frances. "See you later."

Benny put Watch's leash on and the Aldens and Lainey began to walk to town.

As always, everyone they passed said hello.
And as usual, it was very hot. They walked
slowly, and Watch panted a lot.

When they got to Main Street, Lainey
said, "If you want to look around while I
shop, why don't we meet again in an hour?
We can meet in the bookstore."

"Okay," said Henry.

After Lainey had left, Violet said, "Let's
just walk around and look in all the shop
windows."

The Aldens soon discovered that the
town of Elbow Bend wasn't so different
from their hometown of Greenfield. Like
Greenfield, it had a hardware store, an an-
tiques store, a bike shop, a shoe-repair shop,
a pet-supply store, an ice-cream parlor, and
a gift shop.

"Wow," said Benny, "look at all those
cameras!"

They watched as the tourists wandered in
and out of the souvenir and T-shirt shops
and took photographs of one another.

The Aldens decided to walk into the pet
store.

"What a cute dog," said the girl in the store.

"He's hot and thirsty," said Benny.

"Could you let us have a bowl of water for him, please?" asked Violet.

"Sure," said the girl. "I'll go get one right now."

She soon returned with a red bowl filled with water and set it down for Watch. He drank noisily. The Aldens looked around the store.

"You have a nice store," Jessie said.

"Thank you," the girl said. She grinned. "It's not my store, it's my brother's. I just work here so I can get free supplies for Squeeze."

"Squeeze? Who is Squeeze?" asked Henry.

The girl grinned even more broadly and pointed.

The Aldens turned. A large snake was coiled around the branch of a small tree growing out of an enormous pot in the window.

Benny took a step back. "Uh-oh," he said.

The girl said, "Don't worry. Squeeze won't hurt you. He's a boa constrictor and not poisonous. Isn't he beautiful?"

Looking at the snake made Violet nervous, so she looked somewhere else. "Oh," she said. "Look, Watch. Sweaters for dogs!"

"Not that dogs need sweaters very often in this part of the country," the girl commented. "Too hot. They don't usually need those little booties, either. Those are for dogs that live in places with snow, where they put salt on the sidewalk. The salt hurts the dogs' feet. I did sell a set of those booties a few days ago. A whole crowd of people came in the store at once, buying all kinds of things. Some tourists will buy anything!"

Glad to be out of the heat, the Aldens began to look around the store. Benny and Watch took a closer look at Squeeze, being careful not to get *too* close. Henry and Violet bent to study the tropical fish in the big aquarium next to the counter.

Jessie let her eyes wander across the pegboard hung with dog supplies: booties and sweaters, raincoats and fancy collars, in every imaginable color; bones and treats; whistles and toys. . . .

She reached out and picked up a small, thin, silver whistle. She held it up. "About this whistle — " she began.

"Look, there's Lainey!" Benny said. He waved, then dashed to the door and opened it. "Hey, Lainey. We're in here!"

Lainey followed Benny inside the store — and began to scream.

"Nooo!" she shrieked, jumping back and dancing from one foot to the other as if her shoes were on fire. "Eeeek. Oooh! A snaaaaaaake!"

Henry raced over and grabbed Lainey's arm. "This way," he said, and led her outside.

"We'll be right back," Jessie promised. The Aldens all went outside to join Henry and Lainey.

Lainey was pale, with splotches of red on her cheeks. "Sorry," she said. "The snake caught me by surprise. If I'd known it was there, I would never have gone in."

"You *are* afraid of snakes, aren't you?" asked Jessie.

"Terrified," Lainey admitted. "I try not to be, but I can't help it. . . ." Her voice trailed off and she shook her head.

"That's very brave of you to work at the park, then," Violet said, trying to make Lainey feel better.

Lainey managed to smile. "Not so brave. I stick close to the trails and places where I know the snakes aren't likely to be. And I wear big hiking boots that come up almost to my knees. When I had to help out during Stories Under the Stars, I worked in the parking lot directing cars. I didn't even come down to the storytelling until Brad came along to walk with me. That's how afraid I was."

The Aldens exchanged glances. Lainey's confession had just eliminated two of their suspects. There was no way Lainey could have had anything to do with the ghostly dog flitting through the woods around the edges of the storytelling crowd.

"Well, you're safe now," said Henry.

"But if you don't mind," Jessie said, "we'd like to go back into the pet-supply store for a minute."

"Why?" asked Benny.

"You'll see," Jessie said.

Lainey said, "Go on. I'll be at the book-store. See you in a little while."

"Let's go," said Jessie. The Aldens went back into the store and Jessie went straight to the whistle she'd been holding. "I'd like to buy this," she said.

"The silent whistle? Sure," said the girl. She took Jessie's money and counted out the change.

As Jessie slipped the whistle into her pocket, she said casually, "Have you sold any of these lately?"

"Sure," said the girl.

"To the same person who bought the booties?" Jessie asked.

The girl frowned. "I don't know about that. The store was jammed. I just remember selling the booties because it was so un-usual, you know? I *think* it was a lady. But what she looked like, I couldn't tell you. I

remember the booties were white, though. Silly color. Shows dirt."

"Hmmm," said Jessie.

"Thanks for all your help," Violet said. "We really appreciate it."

Jessie nodded. "I think you just helped us solve a mystery."

CHAPTER 8

Setting a Trap

Benny's eyes grew wide. "What?" he gasped.

Jessie didn't answer right away. They went outside and Benny hopped excitedly along next to her.

"We know Lainey's not the one who did it, because she really *is* afraid of snakes, and we know Brad was with her the other night when everyone saw the ghost dog at the storytelling," Henry said. "Is that what you mean?"

"Nope," Jessie said. She held up the

whistle in its package. "This is what I mean. This is a very important clue."

Violet leaned forward and read aloud from the package, " 'Silent dog whistle. You can't hear it, but dogs can. From as far away as a quarter mile or more.' "

"Silent whistle?" Benny asked. "How can a whistle not make any sound?"

"It does make a sound. It's just such a high-pitched sound that only dogs can hear it," Henry said. He was beginning to figure out the mystery, too.

They'd begun to walk back along Main Street.

"Can I try it? Can I blow the whistle?" Benny asked.

"May I," Jessie corrected him automatically, just as Grandfather would have. "Okay, Benny, give it a try."

Benny pulled the whistle from the cardboard and held it to his lips. He blew hard.

No sound came out. But Watch jumped up at Benny, his ears straight up.

Benny blew again. Again no sound came out.

Watch gave a short sharp bark. Across the street, a black Labrador retriever veered sharply and began pulling on his leash as if he wanted to run toward Benny.

"That's enough, Benny," said Jessie.

Violet said, "Wow, it works. It really works. And if you blew the whistle enough, I bet every dog that heard it would start howling and trying to find out who was whistling."

"But who would do it?" Violet asked. "And why?"

"I think whoever did it was the same person who bought the booties. The ground was not damp enough to show any footprints — especially with that person's dog wearing the booties. The dog turned into a ghost!" Jessie told them.

"The girl at the store said she was pretty sure a woman had bought the booties," Violet said. "That means it wasn't Joshua."

"That just leaves Dr. Sage," Henry said.

"I like Dr. Sage," Benny said. "I don't think she's bad."

"But she does have a good reason — she

wants more money for her work. A ghost dog means publicity, and publicity might help her get more money for research," Henry said.

"Who else could it be?" Jessie said.

"Wouldn't the girl in the store know Dr. Sage?" Violet asked.

"Not necessarily. Dr. Sage isn't from around here. And if she went into the store when a bunch of tourists were in there, the girl might not notice her," Jessie argued.

But they didn't get to suspect Dr. Sage much longer. They ran into her coming out of the hardware store.

"Hi, Dr. Sage," said Jessie.

"Found the hole-digger yet?" was her answer.

"Not yet," said Henry. Was this all a clever game Dr. Sage was playing so they wouldn't be suspicious?

"Did you have a nice time at your dinner party?" asked Violet.

"Dinner parties," said Dr. Sage scornfully. "I sat there from eight o'clock until midnight with the mayor and a state senator.

I'd better get some more money for my project, it was so boring!" With that, she stomped away.

Jessie raised her eyebrows. "I guess Dr. Sage really was at the dinner party," she said.

"And that means she couldn't have done it," said Benny.

"We're completely out of suspects," said Henry.

They walked slowly on, not speaking again until they reached the bookstore. Lainey was waiting for them by the front door. "Ready to go home for lunch?" she asked.

"Yes!" said Benny, to no one's surprise.

They began to walk back through town, but Violet stopped and stared at the bookstore window. "Look," she said. "There she is!"

"There who is?" Henry asked.

"The lady who took Kate Frances's picture that first day," Violet said. "The same one who was saying she was going to tell everyone about the ghost dog at Stories Under the Stars the other night. That's her picture on the poster in the corner of the window."

"You're right," Jessie said.

" 'Book signing,' " Henry read from the poster. " 'By Elizabeth Prattle, author of *The Lady and the Midnight Ghost*.' She's here signing books tonight at the bookstore."

"Listen to this." Henry read aloud again, " 'The story of a lady haunted by a special kind of ghost in an old house in the historic town of Ankle Bend.' "

"Ankle Bend?" Violet giggled. "Just like Elbow Bend!"

"It probably *is* Elbow Bend," Lainey said. "She probably just changed the name a little, in case anyone thought they recognized themselves in there."

"Wow," said Violet. "A famous author."

"Not so famous. I think this is her first book, and it's not on any best-seller lists yet that I know about," Lainey said as they began to walk home.

"I guess she knows a lot about ghosts," said Benny. "Maybe that's why she was so upset about the ghost dog."

"That's it! That's it! I have it!" Jessie cried. "Benny! You just solved another mystery!"

"I did?" Benny asked.

Henry looked at Jessie. He said, "I think I know what you're thinking. But we need to prove it . . . and I think I know how!"

"How? Who did it?" Benny almost shouted.

"Here's the plan," said Henry. He looked at Lainey. "And we'll need you and Kate Frances to help us."

"Wow. There sure are a lot of people here," Benny said. It was after dinner, and the Aldens had returned to the bookstore to set their plan in action.

The lady standing next to him said, "Oh, it's because of the ghost! Haven't you heard about it?"

"Sort of," Henry said quickly, in case Benny gave anything away.

"Isn't it amazing? A ghost! Just like in the book!" the woman gushed, clutching her copy of *The Lady and the Midnight Ghost* to her chest.

"There's a ghost dog in the book?" asked Violet.

"Well, no. Actually, it's a horse. But it's almost the same," the woman said. She moved away.

Jessie rolled her eyes.

"Look," Henry said. "Lainey and Kate Frances are talking to her now."

The Aldens edged closer, so they could hear but not be seen by Elizabeth Prattle.

"So we were wondering if you'd like to do a reading, as part of our Stories Under the Stars program. Could you do it tomorrow night? I know it's not much notice, but — "

"Oh, I think I could manage that," Ms. Prattle interrupted. She smiled and signed another book, then turned back to Kate Frances.

"Wonderful," said Kate Frances. "About seven-thirty? You can read and maybe answer questions, and after we take a break you can read some more and then sign books. How does that sound?"

"Fine," said Ms. Prattle. "I'll be there."

"Great," said Kate Frances. "We'll start letting everybody know."

Lainey said, as if it had just occurred to her, "Wow. What if the ghost dog shows up again? Wouldn't that be amazing? I bet people will come just to see if — "

"Lainey, there is *no* ghost dog," Kate Frances said sternly. "Come on, let's get to work."

Ms. Prattle watched them go with a little smile on her lips, and the Aldens watched Ms. Prattle.

CHAPTER 9

Whose Ghost Dog?

"The crowd is just as big for Ms. Prattle as it was for the other story-teller," said Kate Frances. "And nobody even knows her around here." She shook her head before hurrying away to help.

"It's because of the ghost stories. The ghost dog," said Henry.

It was true. As the visitors streamed past them to claim seats in the clearing, they heard snatches of conversation. Almost everyone was talking about the ghost dog.

Then Kate Frances walked onto the stage

to introduce Elizabeth Prattle. The audience fell silent, then cheered as the author walked onstage. She stepped up to the podium, took a sip of water, and smiled. "Welcome to all you believers in good writing — and in ghosts!" she said.

With lots of exaggeration and hand gestures, Ms. Prattle began to read.

No one in the audience seemed to mind the exaggeration. They applauded loudly when Ms. Prattle finished reading, and asked her lots of questions. She talked about how her research had led her to believe that many of the ghost stories she'd heard could be true.

Then it was time for a half-hour break.

Henry slipped his flashlight out of his pocket. "Come on," he said to Violet. "Let's go." He and Violet hurried up the trail toward the parking lot.

People wandered toward the concession stand. Kate Frances and Ms. Prattle walked up the stone steps that divided the two rows of benches where the audience sat to listen. Ms. Prattle stopped and spoke to several people and smiled. But she didn't sign any books. "Not until after it's over," she said. "And don't forget, more books will be for sale!"

The Aldens passed Kate Frances. They knew she was offering to walk with Ms. Prattle. "No, no," said Ms. Prattle. "I need a little time to myself. I'll just walk along the trail and think. Don't worry. I'll be back in time to read again!"

She took a flashlight out of her shoulder bag and moved away up the trail.

Jessie and Benny stayed where they were, watching and waiting.

Nothing happened. A few people drifted back to their seats. Benny whispered, "Where's the ghost dog?"

"I don't know, Benny," said Jessie.

Just then, someone screamed.

"It's the ghost!" a woman shouted.

"The ghost dog!" another voice added.

Even though they'd been expecting it, Benny and Jessie both jumped.

Then they saw it: a white figure moving in and out among the trees.

"Come on!" Jessie said.

She and Benny ran toward the dog, skirting the crowd of people who were trying to back away from it. They dashed to the edge of the woods as the dog disappeared into it.

Jessie pulled the silent whistle from her pocket and raised it to her lips. She blew a blast on it. And then another. And then again.

Benny held his breath.

And then the ghost dog reappeared!

It ran toward them. Then it stopped and turned its head as if listening to something only it could hear. It turned.

Jessie blew harder and harder on the whistle. The dog ran forward, then back, then forward.

Benny ran toward the dog. "Here, dog," he called. "Nice ghost dog!" He pulled a dog biscuit from his pocket and held it out.

The dog stopped at the edge of the shadows. It looked utterly confused. As Benny ran up to it, he saw that it wasn't a ghost dog after all — just a white dog covered with something to make it glow, and wearing booties on its feet.

Pulling a collar with a leash attached to it from his other pocket, Benny slipped the collar over the dog's head. "Good dog," he said. "Good girl."

The dog whined a little and looked anxiously over her shoulder. Then she took the biscuit from Benny's hand and allowed herself to be led out into the light.

"It's a dog!" someone said.

"It's not a ghost at all," said someone else.

Jessie bent to pat the dog.

Just then, Ms. Prattle appeared at the top of the stone steps. The dog saw her and strained on the leash, barking and wagging her tail.

Ms. Prattle walked toward the stage as if she didn't see the dog.

And she really didn't see Henry and Violet following her.

She walked up onto the stage and turned to face the audience. She opened her book, although almost no one was sitting down. Faces turned toward her.

"In this chapter — " Ms. Prattle began.

But she didn't get to continue. Benny let the dog drag him up to the stage. Wagging her tail even harder, the dog jumped up and barked happily at Ms. Prattle.

Ms. Prattle looked down.

Jessie stepped forward. "She's your dog, isn't she?" Jessie asked in a loud clear voice.

"I don't know what you're talking about!" Ms. Prattle said.

Henry said, "We followed you to your car just now, Ms. Prattle. We saw you take your dog out. We saw the whole thing."

Slowly Ms. Prattle closed her book. She nodded. Then she knelt down and held out her arms. "Come here, girl. Come here, Dusty. Good girl," she said. And the dog ran into her arms.

Kate Frances said, "Show's over! Everybody go home."

CHAPTER 10

The Ghost Catchers Explain

The porch swing creaked as Benny and Violet rocked back and forth in it. Curled in the corner, Watch yawned.

It was late, long past dinner, on the last night of the Aldens' visit to Elbow Bend. Mrs. Wade had made another special dinner, almost as good as the first one, with peach cobbler and ice cream for dessert.

Now they were all sitting on the porch, talking about the visit — and about solving the mystery.

"I almost forgot to tell you the good

news," Kate Frances said. "More funding is being given to Dr. Sage's research project."

"Isn't that great?" Lainey added. "That means she can pay Brad to keep working for her and maybe even get a second assistant."

"And I think one of the reasons she got the money was because of all the publicity about the fake ghost dog," said Brad. He'd joined them for dinner and was sitting next to Lainey on the wicker sofa.

"I still can't believe that writer, Elizabeth Prattle, would do all that," said Mrs. Wade. She shook her head. "Some people!"

"She got the idea when she overheard Kate Frances telling ghost stories. That was our first day in Elbow Bend and Kate Frances was giving us a tour of the town," Violet said. "She heard the ghost dog story then, saw how the other tourists reacted. She realized it might be useful to her to help sell her book — since her book is based on the same story."

"And she had her dog with her. Dusty. And Dusty was already trained to come to the silent whistle," Henry added.

"That first night, she just used the whistle as an experiment," Benny said. "That's what made all the dogs bark and howl — except her dog, who's used to the whistle."

"And then she went to Elbow Bend State early in the morning and turned over trash cans and dug holes and planted that dog collar to make it look like a dog had been through there," Violet said.

"And then at Stories Under the Stars, she parked her car away from all the others so no one would see her dog inside," Jessie began.

"But wait," Brad said. "How did she make it glow? And leave no footprints?"

"The glow came from glow-in-the-dark Halloween paint," Violet said. "She washed it off Dusty each time. And she put booties on her dog to keep her from leaving footprints."

"Everybody believed Dusty was a ghost," Jessie said.

"She made the howling by playing a tape recording of a dog howling," added Violet.

"And then, after listening to us talk about

the ghost dog in the parking lot, she decided to make the ghost dog appear in town. So she took her dog to the woods along the back of this house and did the same thing," Jessie said.

"Only this time, Watch tracked Dusty, and we found a spot of wet phosphorescent paint on a tree trunk where Dusty had brushed against it," Henry said. "That's when we knew we weren't chasing a ghost but a real dog."

"But how did you know who did it?" Lainey asked.

Violet blushed a little in the dark, and was glad Lainey couldn't see her.

Jessie said, "We had a few suspects. But we were able to narrow the list down and set a trap."

"And we caught her!" Benny concluded triumphantly.

"You sure did, Benny," said Grandfather.

"She got a lot of publicity," said Kate Frances. "But I don't think it was the kind she wanted."

"Her book is still selling well at the bookstore," said Mrs. Wade. "But I think she's sorry she did what she did."

"She sure left town in a hurry," Kate Frances said. "I don't think she'll try anything like that again."

"Well, it's sure been an exciting visit," Mrs. Wade said. "I hope y'all come again soon."

"We will," said Benny. "And we'll catch more ghosts next time!"

"Oh, Benny," Violet said, and everyone laughed.

GERTRUDE CHANDLER WARNER discovered when she was teaching that many readers who like an exciting story could find no books that were both easy and fun to read. She decided to try to meet this need, and her first book, *The Boxcar Children*, quickly proved she had succeeded.

Miss Warner drew on her own experiences to write the mystery. As a child she spent hours watching trains go by on the tracks opposite her family home. She often dreamed about what it would be like to set up housekeeping in a caboose or freight car — the situation the Alden children find themselves in.

When Miss Warner received requests for more adventures involving Henry, Jessie, Violet, and Benny Alden, she began additional stories. In each, she chose a special setting and introduced unusual or eccentric characters who liked the unpredictable.

While the mystery element is central to each of Miss Warner's books, she never thought of them as strictly juvenile mysteries. She liked to stress the Aldens' independence and resourcefulness and their solid New England devotion to using up and making do. The Aldens go about most of their adventures with as little adult supervision as possible — something else that delights young readers.

Miss Warner lived in Putnam, Connecticut, until her death in 1979. During her lifetime, she received hundreds of letters from girls and boys telling her how much they liked her books.